This book belongs to

_____

Published by Scholastic Inc., 90 Old Sherman Turnpike, Danbury, Connecticut 06816.

ISBN: 0-7172-9960-0

Printed in the U.S.A.

First Scholastic printing, July 2006

THE GIANT THANK-YOU

A Lesson in
Being Thankful

by **Doug Peterson**
Illustrated by **Artful Doodlers**

SCHOLASTIC INC.

New York Toronto London Auckland Sydney
Mexico City New Delhi Hong Kong Buenos Aires

Everyone knows that Vikings did things in **big** ways. They sailed in **vast** ships. They carried **giant** shields. And they threw **huge** parties.

Lyle and Rolf, the two youngest Vikings, were about to set sail on their very first voyage. So to celebrate in style, the rest of the Vikings were throwing an enormous Bon Voyage Blowout for them.

"Thank you so much!" Lyle exclaimed, opening one of his presents. "It's just what I always wanted."

Lyle the Kindly Viking was having loads of fun.
But Rude Rolf was not.

"You call this a gift?" Rolf griped as he opened a
present. "It's a smelly fish."

"It's an air freshener," said Olaf. "Just hang it below
deck, and everything will smell like fresh salmon."

Rolf rolled his eyes and tossed it aside. "Did anybody get me anything good?"

"I did!" chirped Sven. "Open mine next!"

Rolf picked up Sven's present. "Boy, it's big," Rolf said, as a smile began to crack the scowl on his face. "And it's heavy, too!"

Rolf ripped open the present, expecting something huge and expensive like a big-screen TV. "A *fruitcake*?" Rolf said in disbelief. "You gave me a fruitcake?"

"That's right!" said Sven with a big grin. "It's a secret family recipe!"

"But it weighs a ton," growled Rolf.
"What's in it—*cement?*"

Sven's smile melted away.
"Who told you our secret
family recipe?"

As the party went on, Lyle was thankful for each gift—even the ones that weren't exactly what he wanted. But Rolf wasn't thankful for **any** of his gifts.

Rolf piled all the good presents into a cart to take home. And he threw all the bad gifts into a pile marked Rejects.

Just as the last gift was being opened, the town's warning bell sounded.

DING! DONG!

"The giants are coming! The giants are coming!" shouted Harold.

Everyone turned toward the mountains to see two giants heading their way.

The Vikings were very afraid of giants.

"To your battle stations!" shouted Olaf. "We have to find something to fling at them!" Ottar shouted.

Rolf grabbed his fruitcake and chuckled.

"Great idea!" Ottar said with a smile. "We'll clobber 'em with the family recipe!"

"Wait, please!" Lyle suddenly shouted. "I *invited* the giants to the party."

All the Vikings froze—**stunned.**

Lyle explained that the giants were his friends and that he really wanted the giants to be at his party. So the rest of the Vikings allowed the giants to attend the party without being pelted with fruitcake. And much to Rolf's delight, their present was the biggest of them all!

"I can't wait to see what you got us," Lyle told the giants. Lyle tore the paper off the gift to reveal—a **huge**—ball of . . .

... **string?**

"I love it!" Lyle said with glee. "Thank you **SOOOOOO** much!"

The giants smiled. But then Rolf opened his mouth.

"String?" shouted Rolf. "You gave us **string?** What am I gonna do with a big ball of string? This has to be the silliest present of the day!"

Now, it was not usually a good idea to anger giants. But Rolf didn't care.

The giants rumbled and grumbled and looked upset. Then they stomped off angrily.

"Well, I guess that wraps up this party," Rolf said, starting to leave with his cart of good presents. "You can keep the string," he added to Lyle. "And get yourself a giant *cat* to play with it."

"Wait!" Lyle said, as he pushed the ball of string in Rolf's cart. "The giants spent a lot of time making this present, and God wants us to be thankful for **all** our gifts."

"I'll thank you to get **out** of my way," said Rolf, as he headed down the hill.

Suddenly Sven came running toward them, huffing and puffing and carrying the heavy fruitcake. "Wait, Rolf! You forgot to take _my_ gift—"

WHOOOPS!

Sven tripped and the
fruitcake went flying!

The cement-filled cake was so heavy that
when it hit the cart, it sent Rolf and the gifts
rolling down the hill wildly out of control.
The giant ball of string began to unravel
and caught on a tree.

23

Just as Rolf was about to fall over Shortedge Cliff, the ball of string ran out, and he grabbed its end. Although the cart went over, Rolf was saved! The Vikings all looked at one another in amazement and cheered.

Rolf was happy to be safe. As he dusted himself off, he realized that it was the giants' gift that had saved him. Rolf now knew that what counts the most about a gift is the thought behind it. Rolf was sorry for not acting thankful before.

After picking up all the gifts that fell off the cart, Rolf knew exactly what he needed to do next. "We'd better find those giants so that I can thank them **and** tell them I'm sorry," Rolf said to Lyle.

So Lyle and Rolf did just that. They found the giants and showered them with thanks—and Rolf even apologized. Then Lyle and Rolf asked the giants to come back to the party.

Back at the party, everyone continued to celebrate. There was lots of music and food.

As for Rolf, he took the time that night to give *everyone* a great big thank-you.

And as you know, Vikings liked things best
when they were big—especially **thank-yous**.

Let us give thanks to God for his gift. It is so great that no one
can tell how wonderful it really is!

2 Corinthians 9:15